MANNHEIM STEAMROLLER

THE Christmas Angel

A FAMILY STORY

STORY BY CHIP DAVIS
COUPLETS BY NOAH ZACHARY
ILLUSTRATIONS BY JAMES M. TAYLOR

STORY BY CHIP DAVIS
COUPLETS BY NOAH ZACHARY
ILLUSTRATIONS BY JAMES M. TAYLOR

MANNHEIM STEAMROLLER BOOKS
USA

MANNHEIM STEAMROLLER

A FAMILY STORY

Mannheim Steamroller L.L.C.
9130 Mormon Bridge Road, Omaha, NE 68152

ISBN: 0-9754149-1-7

Mannheim Steamroller Books hardcover edition 2004
Manufactured in the United States of America

To my family
Kelly, Evan, Elyse,
Trisha

Villagers Gather, Tree is Lighted

 the village of Hamler, glad hearts were befriended
For the Spirit of hope and goodwill had descended

On children of all ages, their gazes held high
The Eve of Good Christmas was drawing nigh

Amidst all the bustle of holiday fare
As the townsfolk did hurry, their homes to prepare,

They all stopped and marveled at the wonderful sight
Of their very own Christmas Tree, festooned with lights

Each villager hushed to receive tender grace
As a gold Christmas Angel was nestled in place

A loud exclamation arose from the crowd
'Twas a magical sight, one and all did avow

As the villagers bid their evening farewells
No sound could be heard save for tolling church bells

A Young Mother in the Village

 young mother remained to place all of the toys
Underneath the Grand Tree for the girls and the boys

The toys thought of Christmas, that's all they thought of –
When they'd find a new home, and a new child's love

As the church bells tolled twelve, the heart of the night,
The toys under the tree started coming to life!

Soldier Boy, Rag Doll, Snow Boy and Cat,
Teddy and Marion the Marionette

They blinked and they stretched and they rose to their feet
Never was there such a Christmas Eve treat!

The Gargon Arrives
and Takes the Christmas Angel

All of a sudden, a lightning bolt flashed!
And a horrible Creature appeared with a crash!

The Gargon, with cloak as black as the night
And a face that sent tremors of fear and of fright

Spinning madly amidst all the Yule decorations
Spread his distress and his vile devastation

He chased all the toys into hiding and then
Gave a tormenting laugh and started again

Then a glimmer of gold caught his jaundiced eye
And he oozed to the tree and he reached way up high

There at the top of the tree was his prize
The gold Christmas Angel, with fear in her eyes

He pounced on the Angel and held her arms tight
Then he spread his dark cloak
                    and disappeared in the night…

The Young Mother Returns, Sees Damage, Goes into Netherworld

 young mother was about to turn in for the night
When she suddenly felt something wasn't quite right

She returned to the village and fell into despair
At the sight which now greeted her, ruin everywhere

Her heart filled with sadness at such tragedy
But worst of all – the Angel was gone from the tree

Just then she looked up and saw shimmering lights
When she approached, they became ever bright

She moved through the mist and soon found herself hurled
Through a strange, magic place, to a dark Netherworld

Gargon and Souls Dance

In the Darkest of Dark Places, Gargon enthused
Over his new acquisition, his toy to misuse

For the gold Christmas Angel was his to display
He preened and he pranced and he strutted and brayed

His minions, the Lost Souls, could do naught but stare
At the sad little Angel, alone in despair

Toys Rally to Follow the
Young Mother to the Netherworld

eanwhile, the toys finally gathered their might
And set out on their journey, beneath the starlight

With might on their side and faith as their shield
They put on brave faces, their fear to conceal

But the journey was arduous, frightening to all
And the creepy, dark forest did cast a great pall

Soon scary noises from shadows unseen
Turned their courage to jelly, as if it were Halloween

The screech of a hoot owl became the wail of a demon
Each rise in the wind set the toys all to screaming

Angel Spreads her Wings and Dances

 But the spirit of Christmas
inside wasn't dead
And she rose and she danced,
with fanciful wings spread

Gargon Hypnotizes Angel

 The Gargon was angered at this delicate display
And he cast a great spell so the Angel would stay

The Angel resisted, lamenting and wailing
But Gargon persisted, his evil prevailing

They spun and they twirled, all through the night
And finally reached…The Northern Lights

Toys Convince the
Young Mother to Go On

hey raced through the Forest, as fast as toys could
'Til they found the young mother, alone in the wood

She was cold and afraid, her heart full of gloom
The night sky her shroud, her soul but a tomb

The toys knew they must help her, and help her they did
As they gathered around, their own terror they hid

They reminded the mother of what was at stake
The Spirit of Christmas the Gargon did take

But if there was no Christmas then there was no joy
And no wonder or magic for each girl and boy

There would only be daydreams of what might have been
And a sad, empty memory of the Gargon's sin

The young mother's heart would not let it be so
And she stood and she pointed and called out, "No!"

The Young Mother Manages to Transform Gargon

ust then, in the Dark Place, with Christmas half-dead
The Angel managed to lift her sweet head

She waved her wing — dejected, bereft
And spread all of her magic, whatever was left

The young mother was graced with the magic from afar
And was filled with a light like a grand shooting star

She spun around quickly and focused her light
On the Gargon, who tried to flee into the night

But the terrible mask fell away from his face
And a new, kindly visage appeared in its place

For the terrible Gargon was merely thus:
An old Christmas angel, somehow villainous

The magic released the Lost Souls from their jail
And now they were transformed
                                    back into Christmas Angels

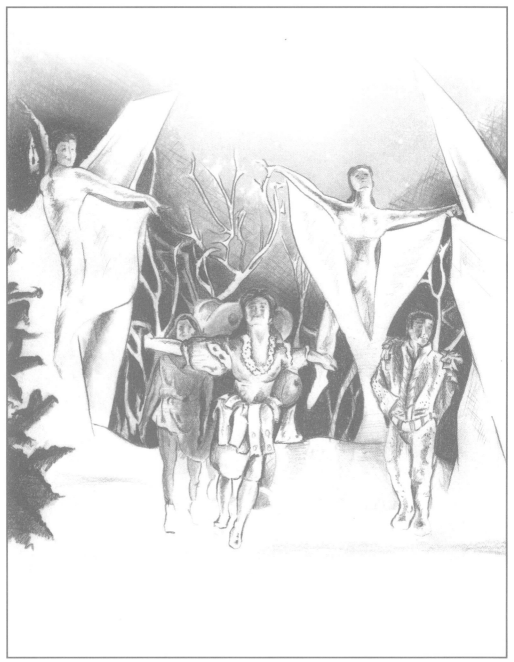

Joy Returns to Netherworld, All Return to Village

he toys all rejoiced at this wonderful turn
They set out at once, their homes to return

Back in the village, they ran to the tree
And jumped back to their places, merry with glee

The children woke up and found, to their delight
The toys which had such adventures last night

And the gold Christmas Angel, on branches so tall
Spread her wings and gave magic to one and all

Joy and goodwill came to everyone's soul
Through the magic of Christmas and an Angel of Gold

For more Mannheim Steamroller brand
music products, books, and concert tour schedules

visit our website
www.mannheimsteamroller.com
or call us at 402-457-4341